#5

MY BOYFRIEND IS A MONSTER

I Date Dead People

OR

MY BOYFRIEND IS SO TRANSPARENT

OR

MY SO-CALLED AFTERLIFE

OR

YOUR MEMORY STILL HAUNTS ME

OR

SOUL MATES

OR

I LOVE BOO

ANN KERNS

Illustrated by JANINA GÖRRISSEN

STORY BY
ANN KERNS

ILLUSTRATIONS BY
JANINA GÖRRISSEN

WITH ADDITIONAL INKS BY
MARC RUEDA

LETTERING AND COVER COLORING BY
ELDON COWGUR

Graphic Universe™
A division of Lerner Publishing Group, Inc.
241 First Avenue North
Minneapolis, MN 55401 U.S.A.

Website address: www.lernerbooks.com

Main body text set in CC MildMannered 7/7.5.
Typeface provided by Comicraft/Active Images.

Library of Congress Cataloging-in-Publication Data

Kerns, Ann, 1959–
I date dead people / by Ann Kerns ; illustrated by Janina Görrissen.
p. cm. — (My boyfriend is a monster ; #5)
Summary: The renovation of Nora's old Victorian house unearths a teenaged poltergeist who falls in love with Nora, causing more ghosts to appear and Nora's parents to become quite unhappy.
ISBN: 978–0–7613–6007–0 (lib. bdg. : alk. paper)
1. Graphic novels. [1. Graphic novels. 2. Ghosts—Fiction. 3. Dating (Social customs)—Fiction. 4. High schools—Fiction. 5. Schools—Fiction.] I. Görrissen, Janina, ill. II. Title.
PZ7.7.K46Iam 2012
741.5'973—dc23 2011021542

Manufactured in the United States of America
1 – BC – 12/31/11

Chapter 1:
AUTUMN'S GHOSTS
THE REILLY FAMILY HOME.
ST. PAUL, MINNESOTA.
EARLY OCTOBER.
NEILSON
Historic Renovations

World's Best HONEY BOMBS
MOM, I'M TOO OLD FOR STEP DANCING. IT'S MAKING MY CALVES ENORMOUS.
BESIDES, DRAMA CLUB WILL KEEP ME BUSY ALL YEAR.
CREAM, NO SUGAR, RIGHT?
THANKS, BILL.
BUT, NORA, YOU LOOK SO PRETTY IN YOUR COSTUME!
I LOOK LIKE A ST. PATRICK'S DAY CARD.
IT'S TIME FOR EILEEN TO SUFFER FOR OUR HERITAGE. I'M OUT.
FUN HOOPS

HOW ABOUT IT, BEAN?
DO YOU WANT TO SUFFER FOR OUR HERITAGE?
OKAY.
BEAN, DID DADDY BRAID YOUR HAIR?
NO.
INGE DID IT.
INGE?
WHO'S INGE, HONEY?
THE MAID.
AH, I DIDN'T KNOW WE HAD A MAID.
WELL, SHE DID A VERY GOOD JOB ON YOUR HAIR.
HEY, AID, DID YOU TAKE MY IPOD?
YEAH, I TOOK YOUR IPOD CUZ I WANNA LISTEN TO *YOUR* MUSIC.
World's Best HONEY BOMBS
World's Best FUN HOOPS

MORNING, ALL.
HOW'S THE COFFEE, BOYS?
HI, DADDY.
JIM, DID YOU CALL THE HAYS SOCIETY ABOUT THE GRANDFATHER CLOCK?
WHAT ABOUT THE CLOCK?
HONEY BOMBS
WE'RE DONATING IT TO THE ELEANOR HAYS LITERARY SOCIETY.
IT BELONGED TO HER WHEN SHE LIVED HERE--
FUN HOOPS
SLAAAM!!

WHOA.
WINDY OUT THERE.

I GOTTA GO.
ME TOO.
KIRSTY WILL BE HERE ANY MINUTE.

IT WASN'T THE WIND.

IT *WASN'T* THE *WIND.*
WHY DOESN'T ANYONE SEE THAT?

WHAT ARE YOU TALKING ABOUT?
NEVER MIND!

AND THEN I WANT TO PAINT ONE WALL LIKE A REALLY SOFT LAVENDER. I HAVE A BUNCH OF FURNITURE MARKED IN A CATALOG.
I'LL SHOW YOU AFTER SCHOOL, KIRSTY. I NEED YOUR OPINION.
COOL.
I'M SO HAPPY YOU MOVED INTO THE NEIGHBORHOOD.
I WAS NERVOUS ABOUT STARTING AT A NEW SCHOOL, BUT YOU AND JAMILA HAVE BEEN AMAZING.
YOU'RE SO LUCKY!
YOUR HOUSE IS LIKE A FAMOUS LITERARY LANDMARK.
HEY, WHAT IF YOU DISCOVER SOME OF ELEANOR HAYS'S PAPERS HIDDEN SOMEWHERE?!
LIKE AN UNPUBLISHED NOVEL. OR A DIARY!
WHAT IF YOU FIND OUT THAT SHE HAD SOME GREAT LOVE THAT SHE KEPT A SECRET?!
THAT WOULD BE SOOO ROMANTIC.

ALL THOSE YEARS SHE LIVED ALONE--IT WAS BECAUSE SHE COULDN'T FORGET HER LOST LOVE.
MAYBE HE WAS KILLED A LONG TIME AGO, LIKE IN VIETNAM.
OR MAYBE HER FAMILY DIDN'T APPROVE OF HIM.
STOP
KIRSTY, YOU HAVE NO IDEA HOW MUCH I WISH I'D LIVED IN THE PAST.
GUYS NOWADAYS--PFFFT.
THEY'RE SO CHILDISH.
DON'T YOU WISH WE LIVED BACK IN ELEANOR'S TIME?
OR BETTER YET, WAY BACK IN JANE AUSTEN'S TIME?
I THINK I'M HAPPY JUST READING ABOUT IT.

I'LL NEVER FIND A MR. DARCY OR A HEATHCLIFF IN THIS WORLD.
THERE ARE SOME CUTE BOYS AT SCHOOL...

THERE'S ONE NOW.
WHO?

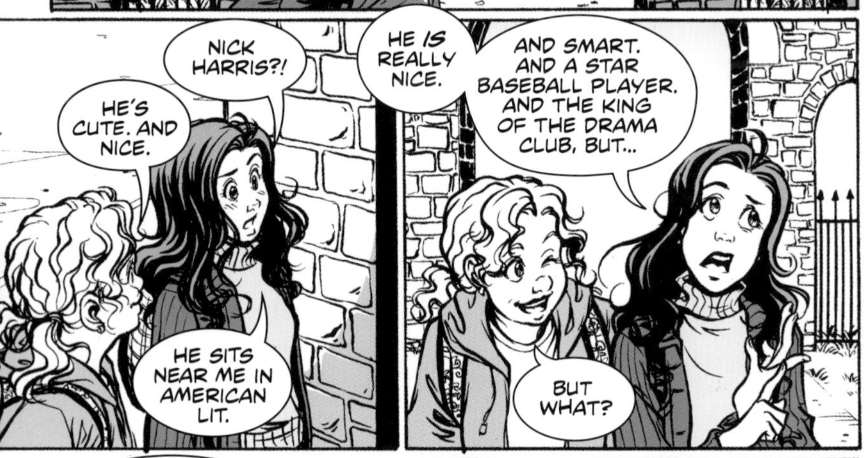
HE'S CUTE. AND NICE.
NICK HARRIS?!
HE SITS NEAR ME IN AMERICAN LIT.
HE *IS* REALLY NICE.
AND SMART. AND A STAR BASEBALL PLAYER. AND THE KING OF THE DRAMA CLUB, BUT...
BUT WHAT?

KIRSTY, A GUY LIKE NICK WOULDN'T GIVE ME A SECOND THOUGHT.
I MIGHT AS WELL BE INVISIBLE.

DO YOU REALLY THINK THAT?
I KNOW IT.

I HAVE TO SEE MR. BARRY THIS MORNING.
HE WANTS TO MAKE SURE I'M ADJUSTING SUCCESSFULLY.
OH, GOOD LUCK WITH THAT.
I'LL SEE YOU AT LUNCH?
YEP.
SEE YA!

HEY, NORA...
HI!

THERE YOU ARE, NORA. WELCOME, WELCOME.
MR. HARRIS, DID YOU NEED SOMETHING?
NO, JUST, YOU KNOW, ON MY WAY TO CLASS.
ALL RIGHT THEN.
WELL, COME ON IN, NORA.
SHE DOESN'T EVEN NOTICE ME.
AM I INVISIBLE?

OH...MY...BLUE... HEAVEN. HERE'S BIG JIM WEARING A PLAID SHIRT WITH HIS HAIR IN A PONYTAIL.
OH, YEAH. MY DAD WAS A TOTAL HEADBANGER.
HILARIOUS. AND IS THIS YOUR MOM?
DUDE, YOU LOOK JUST LIKE HER. DOESN'T SHE, JJ?
LET'S SEE.
WERE YOU NOT JUST SITTING BEHIND ME ON THE BED?
NO. I WAS AT THE CLOSET.
WOW. THAT WAS WEIRD.
I COULD'VE SWORN YOU--
LET ME SEE THE PICTURE.
WHAT?
OH, YEAH. HERE.

YOUR PARENTS WERE SO COOL.
HOW DID THEY MEET?
AT A CONCERT AT FIRST AVENUE IN MINNEAPOLIS.
QUINN JAMES! WHA--?!
WAIT, DIDN'T I TELL YOU GUYS?
MY DAD KNEW MR. JAMES IN COLLEGE!
GET OUT!
I KNOW!
I COULDN'T BELIEVE IT WHEN IT TURNED OUT THAT MR. JAMES WAS THE DRAMA CLUB ADVISOR.
I THINK HE STILL HAS THAT SWEATER VEST.
SHOOT, IT'S ALMOST 5! I GOTTA GO!
I SHOULD GO TOO.
MY GRANDPARENTS ARE COMING FOR DINNER.

ARE YOU GOING TO THE BOYS' GAME TONIGHT, NORA?
NAH.
YOU'RE A MUCH NICER BIG SISTER THAN ME.
I'M LOOKING FORWARD TO HAVING THE HOUSE TO MYSELF.
GIVE ME A CALL LATER IF YOU GET BORED.
SEE YA, NORA!
GONG
AH!
GONG GONG GONG GONG
MAN, I'LL BE GLAD WHEN THEY CART YOU OFF.

Chapter 2:
BEYOND
BEYOND ALL THAT WE KNOW
ALL THAT WE SEE
THERE'S ANOTHER WORLD
A FARTHER ROOM...

HELLO?
DAD, IS THAT YOU?

ARE YOU GUYS HOME ALREADY?
DAD?
MOM?

BEYOND ALL THAT WE KNOW
ALL THAT WE SEE
THERE'S ANOTHER WORLD
A FARTHER ROOM...

DAD?
THAT'S...
NOT YOU...

WHAT SHOULD I DO?
CALL THE POLICE.
CALL THE POLICE.
MY PHONE'S DOWNSTAIRS.

OKAY, CALM DOWN.
WHY WOULD A BURGLAR BE SINGING?
I'M IMAGINING IT.

OKAY...
ONE, TWO, THREE--

MY PARENTS COULD'VE BOUGHT A NICE *NEW* HOUSE IN THE SUBURBS.
BUT OH, NO, THEY HAD TO MOVE US INTO THE CREAKIEST, SHADOWIEST HOUSE THEY COULD FIND.
IS SHADOWIEST EVEN A WORD?

AND NEXT TIME, GENIUS, BRING YOUR PHONE UPSTAIRS WITH YOU.

CREAK
AAAHHH!

AAAHHHH!
WHAT DO YOU WANT?
YOU CAN SEE ME?
UH-HUH.
AND YOU CAN HEAR ME?
OBVIOUSLY.
DON'T MOVE THE CLOCK.

HEY!
YOU WERE SINGING BEFORE...
DID YOU STEAL MY IPOD?
I WANT IT BACK!

WHERE HAVE YOU GUYS BEEN?!
NORA, WHAT ARE YOU DOING SITTING OUTSIDE?
IT'S CHILLY OUT HERE!
I'M FINE.
I'M NOT...
I'M FINE.
I'M JUST...
YOU KNOW, THAT HOUSE CAN BE PRETTY CREEPY SOMETIMES.
AND I DON'T THINK WE SHOULD GIVE THAT CLOCK AWAY.
I THINK THAT WOULD BE...
DANGEROUS.
COME ON INSIDE, HONEY.

THIS IS NICE, ISN'T IT?
MMMM...
THERE ARE VERY FEW THINGS THAT CAN'T BE SOLVED WITH HOT CHOCOLATE AND MARSHMALLOWS.
WHAT AM I SITTING ON?
YOU THINK I WAS ACTING PRETTY CRAZY BEFORE, HUH?
I JUST WANT TO MAKE SURE YOU'RE OKAY.
NEW SCHOOL. NEW--

NO ONE LIVES ANY NEARER THAN TOWN. NO ONE...
AAAAH!
YIKES!

I DON'T KNOW WHAT'S WRONG WITH THIS TV.
THE COMPUTER TOO.
AIDAN SAYS HIS VIDEO GAMES ARE MESSED UP.
HE SAYS STRANGE NAMES KEEP POPPING UP ON THE PLAYER LIST.
WE SHOULD HAVE THE ELECTRICIAN LOOK AT--
THANKS FOR THE HOT CHOCOLATE.
LOVE YOU. G'NIGHT.
UM... OKAY.
GOOD NIGHT, HONEY.
MAYBE WE NEED A NEW TV.

COME ON, YOU.
Kittens go Crazy
GOT A MINUTE, BEAN?
WHAT ARE WE DOING?
YEAH, WHAT'S GOING ON?

THAT'S WHAT I'D LIKE TO KNOW.
YOU TWO KNOW ABOUT THE GHOST, DON'T YOU?

YOU SAW SOMETHING?

YES!
THE GHOST CHASED ME UP THE STAIRS TONIGHT!

WHICH ONE?

THE *FRONT* STAIRS.

NO, WHICH GHOST?
THERE WAS ONLY ONE GHOST.
HE'S A BOY, ABOUT MY AGE.
HE TALKED TO ME.
HE'S-- HE'S A LITTLE UPSET THAT WE'RE MOVING THINGS AROUND. LIKE GHOSTS GET.
BUT OTHERWISE, HE SEEMED PRETTY NORMAL.
AS DISEMBODIED ENTITIES GO.
SO NEXT TIME, MAYBE JUST TRY TALKING TO HIM. MAKE HIM FEEL MORE RELAXED.
OH, YEAH, I'LL TRY TO MAKE HIM FEEL AT HOME.

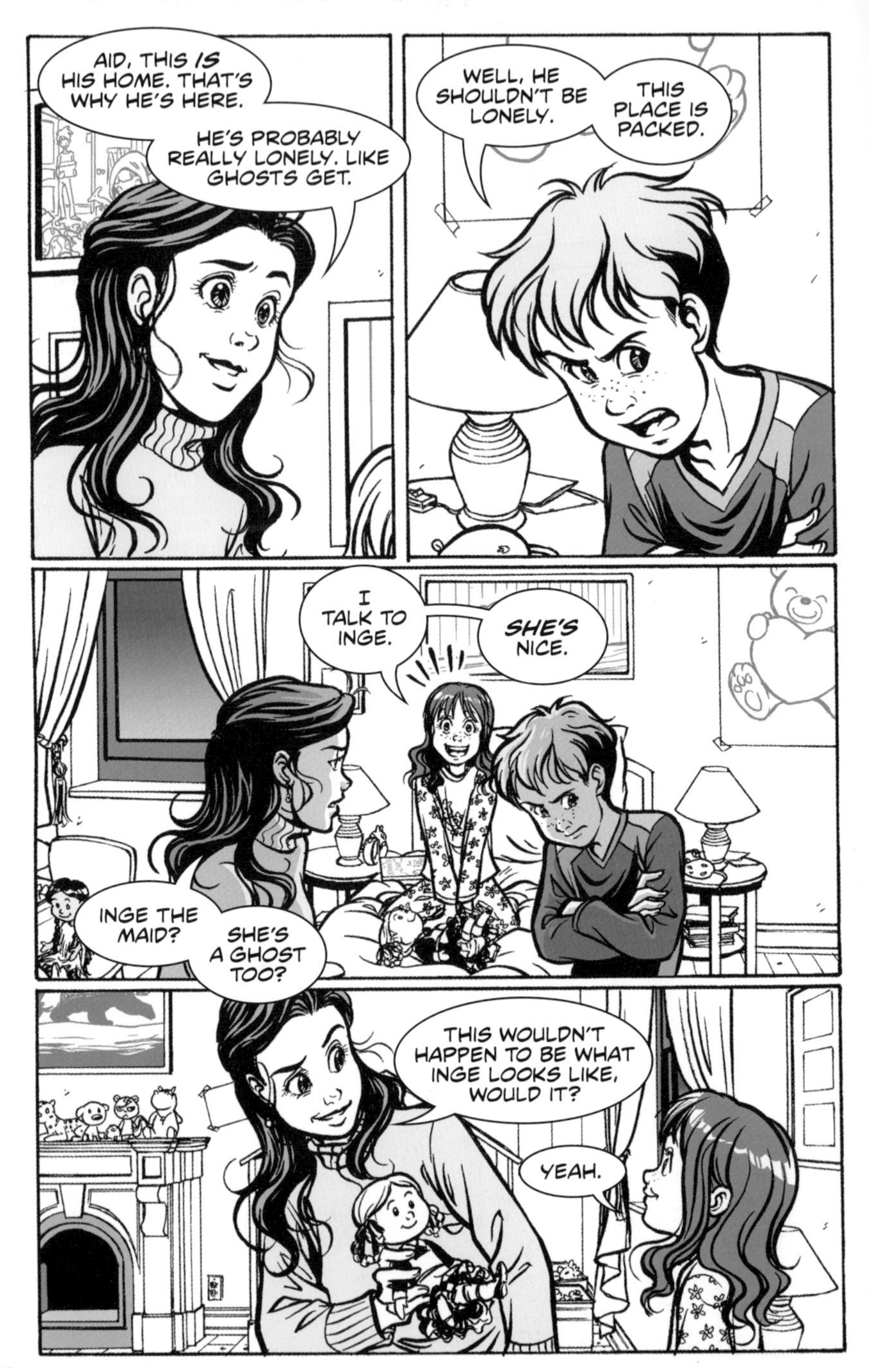
AID, THIS *IS* HIS HOME. THAT'S WHY HE'S HERE.
HE'S PROBABLY REALLY LONELY. LIKE GHOSTS GET.
WELL, HE SHOULDN'T BE LONELY.
THIS PLACE IS PACKED.
I TALK TO INGE.
SHE'S NICE.
INGE THE MAID?
SHE'S A GHOST TOO?
THIS WOULDN'T HAPPEN TO BE WHAT INGE LOOKS LIKE, WOULD IT?
YEAH.

EILEEN, WE'RE NOT TALKING ABOUT PRETEND NOW.
I KNOW!
THE GHOSTS AREN'T NICE!
I DON'T WANT TO TALK TO THEM OR MAKE THEM FEEL BETTER.
I WANT THEM TO GO AWAY!
AIDAN, IF HE WAS SCARING YOU, WHY DIDN'T YOU TELL ME ABOUT THE GHOST BEFORE?
THEY TOLD US NOT TO TELL.
THEY SAID IT WAS A SECRET.
HE TOLD ME HE'D GET US IF WE TOLD.
THE TALL ONE SAID THEY COULD TAKE US WITH THEM AND WE'D NEVER SEE MOM AND DAD AGAIN.

WHAT?
HE THREATENED YOU?!

I'LL TAKE CARE OF THIS.

AID, TAKE EILEEN BACK TO YOUR ROOM, OKAY?
READ TO HER OR SOMETHING.

I'M GOING TO HAVE A WORD WITH OUR LOST SOUL.

HM.
THREATEN MY FAMILY, WILL YOU?
DEEP BREATH.
YOU'RE NOT AFRAID OF HIM.

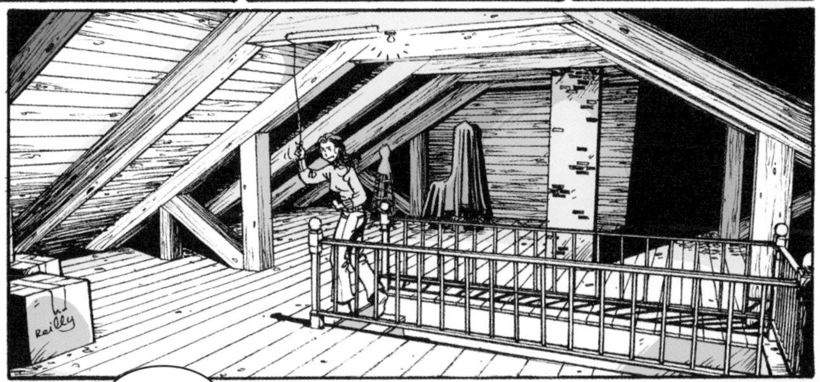
Reilly

HEY!
GHOST!
YOU *ARE* UP HERE, AREN'T YOU?
DON'T GHOSTS ALWAYS HIDE IN ATTICS?
IN THE CREEPIEST, SHADOWIEST ROOM IN THE HOUSE?

THAT IS, WHEN YOU'RE NOT THREATENING LITTLE KIDS?
SHOW YOURSELF!

HOW DARE YOU SCARE THEM LIKE THAT?
I DON'T CARE WHO YOU ARE OR WHAT YOUR SAD STORY IS.
YOU STAY AWAY FROM THOSE KIDS!
IF YOU HAVE SOMETHING TO SAY, YOU CAN SAY IT TO--
PLINK
UMPFF
OW.

HE WON'T KNOW WHERE I AM...
...THINK THEY'RE BETTER THAN ME...
WHO'S THERE?
...TOSS US OUT ONTO THE STREET...
STOP IT!
STOP IT!
...TRAPPED FOREVER...
WE MISS YOU SO MUCH...
WHO'S IN THE HOUSE WITH US?

AAAAH!!!
WHAT'S WRONG WITH YOU?
WHAT'S WRONG WITH ME? YOU'RE WHAT'S WRONG.
YOU KNOCKED ME DOWN!
I WOULD NEVER STRIKE A LADY.

OH, YEAH. I SUPPOSE IT WAS SOME OTHER GH--

OH, WOW.
THE OTHER GHOSTS?

I DON'T KNOW WHO STRUCK YOU.
BUT I AM NOT ALONE.
WAIT!
HOW MANY OF YOU ARE THERE?

I AM NOT ONE OF *THEM.*
AND I DON'T KNOW HOW MANY THERE ARE.
TWO, THREE.
MAYBE MORE.
YOU DON'T KNOW? HOW CAN YOU NOT KNOW?
THEY AREN'T EXACTLY CHATTY.
WILL YOU PLEASE STOP AND TALK TO ME?
I NEED SOME ANSWERS!
PHOTOS
NOW!
PLEASE.

SORRY. I JUST--
YOU ARE A VERY MODERN YOUNG WOMAN.
NO ONE'S EVER ACCUSED ME OF THAT BEFORE.

THESE OTHER GHOSTS...
YOU CAN'T SEE THEM?
WHY?
IT'S HARD TO EXPLAIN. THIS... EXISTENCE...IT'S LIKE PASSING IN AND OUT OF TIME.
I'VE LEARNED TO CONTROL WHEN I APPEAR.
BUT I CAN'T CONTROL THE OTHERS. IF THEY WANT TO HIDE FROM ME...

PLEASE SIT.
I HAVEN'T EVEN ASKED YOU YOUR NAME.
THOMAS BARNES.
MY FRIENDS CALL--CALLED ME TOM.
MY NAME IS NORA.
YES, I KNOW.
YOU LISTEN IN ON US, DON'T YOU?
YOU HEARD US TALKING ABOUT THE CLOCK.
I DON'T KNOW IF I'M GOING TO BE ABLE TO STOP THEM FROM GIVING AWAY THE CLOCK.
THEY PROMISED IT TO THE HAYS SOCIETY AND--

IT BELONGS TO MY FAMILY.
ELEANOR HAYS WAS MY GREAT-NIECE.
SHE WAS?
THESE ARE YOUR FRIENDS? KIRSTY AND JAMILA?
YES. AT THE STATE FAIR THIS SUMMER.
I LIKE YOUR FRIENDS. THEY'RE VERY CLEVER. AND AMUSING.

YOU WERE IN THE ROOM THE OTHER DAY, WEREN'T YOU?
WHEN WE WERE LOOKING AT PICTURES?
YES. YOUR FATHER WAS A *HEADBANGER.*
I LIKE THE WAY ALL OF YOU TALK. IT MAKES ME LAUGH.

SO GHOSTS LAUGH?
I DO.
SOMETIMES.
NOW.
NOW?
THIS HOUSE WAS VERY QUIET BEFORE.
FOR DECADES, ONLY ELEANOR LIVED HERE. SHE SPENT MOST OF HER TIME WRITING.
CAN I ASK YOU SOMETHING?
WHY ARE YOU HERE?
YOU ORDERED ME IN AND SHUT THE DOOR.
NO, I MEAN, WHY DIDN'T YOU... PASS ON? THE NEXT WORLD. THAT.
I WAS WORRIED ABOUT MY PARENTS.
...ON MY UNCLE'S FARM NEAR LE SUEUR...
I BROKE MY NECK.
I DIED AT ONCE.
I WAS EIGHTEEN.
I'M STILL EIGHTEEN.

THE NEXT THING I KNEW, I WAS BACK HERE AT THE HOUSE.
MY PARENTS AND MY SISTER WERE TERRIBLY UPSET.
I TRIED TO TELL MY MOTHER THAT I WAS ALL RIGHT.
BUT SHE COULDN'T HEAR ME. NO ONE COULD.
SO I STAYED, TO WATCH OVER THEM.
AND THEN ONE DAY, I HEARD THEM ALL IN THE GARDEN. MY SISTER HAD GOTTEN ENGAGED.
MY *LITTLE SISTER.*
WITH A YOUNG MAN, IN LOVE.
THEY WERE HAPPY AGAIN.
I REALIZED THAT THEY HAD MOVED ON.
I KNEW THAT I SHOULD TOO. BUT I COULDN'T.
I COULDN'T FIND MY WAY OUT.
IT WAS AS IF A DOOR HAD CLOSED.

OH, WOW.
YOU WERE TRAPPED IN THE HOUSE.
YES.
IT WAS...NOT "SO COOL."
I LEARNED TO BE A PROPER GHOST.
MY GREAT-NIECE ELEANOR COULD HEAR ME. AND SOMETIMES SEE ME.
AND NOW I CAN HEAR AND SEE YOU.
YES.

I ALWAYS IMAGINED THAT A GHOST WOULD BE...
I DON'T KNOW, LIKE A MIST.
BUT YOU SEEM SO REAL.
YOU CAN TOUCH THINGS.
WHAT DOES IT FEEL LIKE TO TOUCH YOU? COULD I...

OOPS, I MISSED.
BUT IT FELT AMAZING. LIKE...
LIKE A COOL SPARK.
LIKE A SPARK.
TRY AGAIN.
WHEN I FIRST LEARNED TO PICK THINGS UP, I HAD TO CONCENTRATE VERY HARD.
OKAY, CONCENTRATE.

WE'LL HAVE TO KEEP PRACTICING *THAT.*
I WOULD BE WILLING TO DO THAT.
LIKE A COOL SPARK.
DID YOU WANT TO SEE MORE PHOTOS?
I HAVE TONS OF ALBUMS.
I WOULD LIKE TO SEE PHOTOS, BUT...
WOULD YOU SHOW ME WHAT YOU WRITE?
YOU MEAN YOU DON'T JUST LOOK AT THEM WHEN I'M NOT HERE?
I WOULD NEVER DO THAT.

02:09
SO IT WAS REALLY LIKE THAT BACK THEN?
YOU JUST SAT IN HER FRONT PARLOR?
WITH HER PARENTS RIGHT THERE?
AND THAT WAS A *DATE?*
YES.
I COULD NEVER HAVE TALKED TO HER LIKE THIS.
SO EASILY.
SHE WAS NOTHING LIKE YOU. NONE OF THEM WERE.
NONE OF THEM?
WELL, THERE WERE ONLY SEVEN OR EIGHT.
ONLY?

IS THAT CLOCK RIGHT?
!
I SHOULD GO.

YOU WILL APOLOGIZE TO YOUR BROTHER FOR ME ABOUT THE COMPUTER GAMES?
YES, I WILL.

SEE YOU TOMORROW.
GOOD NIGHT.

WHOA.

BEYOND ALL THAT WE LOVE...
ALL THAT WE NEED...

THERE'S ANOTHER...
CALLING OUT...

Chapter 3:
HERE NOW
William Shakespeare's
As You Like It

THERE YOU GO, ALEX. ALL SET.
THANKS, KATHY.
ACTUALLY, MY NAME IS *KIRSTY*.
I'LL NEVER GET THE LEAD WHILE SHE'S HERE.
ALEX CAN'T GET *ALL* THE LEAD ROLES.
SHE CAN! MR. JAMES LOVES HER.
WELL, SHE IS REALLY TALENTED. SINGING, DANCING, ACTING.
AND FACE IT--NONE OF THE POPULAR BOYS WOULD BE IN DRAMA CLUB IF IT WEREN'T FOR ALEX.
IT'S NOT FAIR.
SHE'S SETTING MY CAREER BACK TWO YEARS, AT LEAST.

YOU'LL GET A LEAD BEFORE WE GRADUATE.
YOU'RE A GREAT ACTOR.
YOU JUST HAVE MORE COMPETITION HERE THAN YOU HAD IN JUNIOR HIGH.
YOU'RE SO CALM ABOUT IT. DON'T YOU EVEN WANT A LEAD?
ME?
NO, I'M HAVING FUN JUST BEING AN EXTRA.
HEY, KIRSTY, CAN I GET A PIC OF YOU WORKING ON A COSTUME?

HOW ABOUT YOU AND NORA GO STAND IN THE BACK BY THE GREEN ROOM?
IN FRONT OF THE BIG WINDOWS?
SERIOUSLY.
AM I INVISIBLE?

WHERE DID BRANDON GO?
I DON'T KNOW. HE WAS JUST HERE.
I'LL GO FIND HIM.
WOW.

HI.
HI.
HI.
ARE YOU LOOKING FOR SOMEONE?
YES.

WHAT?
WHO?
WHO ARE YOU LOOKING FOR?
RIGHT.
KIRSTY. I RIPPED THE SLEEVE ON MY SHIRT.
SHE'LL BE BACK IN A MINUTE.
I'M NORA, BY THE WAY.
YEAH, I KNOW.
YOU'RE IN MY LIT CLASS.
AM I?
I MEAN, I AM.
I DIDN'T THINK YOU KNEW THAT.

HEY, I HEARD YOU TALKING THE OTHER DAY ABOUT THAT OLD MOVIE. *THE LAST OF THE MOHICANS.*
YEAH, SO I WATCHED IT.
IT WAS GREAT!
ISN'T IT? I LOVE THAT MOVIE.
SO...
I WAS WONDERING IF YOU'RE GOING TO THE BONFIRE ON FRIDAY.
MAYBE WE COULD GO TOGETHER.
ARE YOU ASKING ME OUT, NICK?
WHY, YES, NORA, I AM.

UM, I CAN'T.
I THINK I'M...SEEING SOMEONE.
OH, LIKE, DATING?
OH. I DIDN'T KNOW THAT.
WHO IS IT?
SOMEONE FROM YOUR OLD SCHOOL?
WELL, UH, HE *IS* SOMEONE FROM THE PAST...
I FOUND BRANDON.
ARE WE READY FOR OUR CLOSE-UP?
JUST...
RIGHT IN THAT LIGHT...
THAT'LL BE PERFECT.

SLUMMING WITH THE NERDS, NICK?
EVERYONE'S NOTICED YOU CHASING AFTER THE NEW GIRL.
WHAT COULD SOMEONE LIKE *YOU* POSSIBLY SEE IN *HER*?
DON'T BE BORING, ALEX.
MAYBE I LIKE HER BECAUSE SHE TALKS ABOUT SOMETHING OTHER THAN HOW MUCH HER SHOES COST.
OR MAYBE IT'S THAT SHE DOESN'T SAY THINGS LIKE, "SLUMMING WITH THE NERDS."
SERIOUSLY?
CRANKY.

HANGING WITH THE DRAMA CLUB ROYALTY, NORA?
AND WHAT WERE YOU AND NICK HARRIS CHATTING ABOUT?
OH, NOTHING.
WELL, HE ASKED ME OUT.
I KNEW IT! I TOLD YOU!
WHERE ARE YOU GOING?
WE'RE NOT GOING ANYWHERE.
I SAID NO.
YOU WHAT NOW?
KIRSTY, I HAVE TO TELL YOU SOMETHING.
SOMETHING WEIRD.

A GHOST?
YOU'RE DATING A GHOST?
THAT IS *SO* COOL.
KIRSTY, YOU FELT HIM THE OTHER DAY.
HE WAS SITTING BEHIND YOU ON MY BED.
HIS NAME IS TOM.
I *KNEW* THERE WAS SOMEONE BEHIND ME.
IS HE CUTE?
SERIOUSLY, JJ, *THAT'S* THE ONE QUESTION YOU HAVE?
IT'S NOT THE *ONLY* QUESTION.
IT'S JUST THE MOST *IMPORTANT* ONE.

HE IS CUTE.
AND VERY SWEET.
AND SMART.
AND YOU TURNED DOWN A DATE WITH NICK HARRIS...
...NICK HARRIS, WHO IS NOT ONLY *ALIVE* BUT IS, LIKE, THE COOLEST GUY IN THE SCHOOL.
...BECAUSE OF THIS GHOST?
CAN YOU KISS A GHOST?
KIRSTY, WE DON'T CHOOSE THE PEOPLE WE FALL IN LOVE WITH.
YES. YES, WE DO.
EXCEPT IN ROMANCE NOVELS...
MAYBE THIS TIME LIFE *IS* LIKE A ROMANCE NOVEL.
MAYBE, WHEN LIFE GIVES US ROMANCE, WE HAVE TO *TAKE IT.*

SO IF THIS TOM DOES EXIST AND YOU HAVEN'T TOTALLY LOST YOUR MIND...HE ISN'T EVEN THE ONLY GHOST IN THE HOUSE?
WHY HAVEN'T YOU TOLD YOUR PARENTS ABOUT THIS?
TELL HER PARENTS?
ARE YOU SERIOUS?
MY PARENTS ALWAYS HAVE TO SOLVE THINGS.
I DON'T WANT THEM TO *SOLVE* TOM.
WHY DON'T YOU COME OVER TONIGHT?
YOU'LL SEE THAT TOM'S REAL...
...AND THAT HE'S GREAT!
AND AFTER WE MEET TOM...
YOU'LL TELL YOUR PARENTS ABOUT THE OTHER ONES.
YES!
I'M SO THERE.

Chapter 4:
PROOF
HISSSSSSS!!
REEE-OONWWWWW!

SO THAT'S WHEN WE FOUND OUT THAT JIM--YOUR DAD--COULDN'T SWIM.
HONESTLY, JEAN, I DON'T KNOW HOW YOUR MOTHER PUT UP WITH US THAT SUMMER AT THE CABIN.
OH, SHE LOVED IT.
SHE THRIVED ON A FULL HOUSE AND--
FSST
MEOORRW
WHAT ON EARTH?!
REEORW
I HAVEN'T SEEN THOSE TWO BAGS OF BONES MOVE THAT FAST IN YEARS.
SOMETHING SPOOKED THE POOR BEASTS.

MOM, CAN WE TAKE OUR CAKE UPSTAIRS?
YOU CAN AS SOON AS YOU HELP ME CLEAR THE TABLE.
NO, QUINN, YOU SIT DOWN.
THUMP THUMP THUMP THUMP
CATS, JUST CATS.
HOW MUCH DO THOSE CATS WEIGH?
HOPE YOU DIDN'T MIND TAKOUT FOR DINNER, QUINN.
THE KITCHEN'S A BIT OF A DISASTER.
BUT THE COFFEE'S HOMEMADE.
DINNER WAS GREAT.
I CAN'T TELL YOU HOW MUCH IT MEANS TO ME TO BE HERE AMONG FRIENDS.
YOU'VE HAD A RUN OF BAD LUCK.
WE WERE REALLY WORRIED WHEN WE GOT THAT E-MAIL FROM YOU IN NEW MEXICO. AND THE ONE FROM FLORIDA.
AND THEN... WHAT WAS IT... ALASKA?
WELL, IT'S ALL OVER NOW.
HERE'S TO BETTER LUCK IN GOOD OLD ORDINARY ST. PAUL!

I AM SO EXCITED!
I'VE NEVER MET A GHOST BEFORE!
YOU'LL LOVE TOM. HE'S--
PRIDE & PREJUDICE
SLAM!
WHICH ONE OF THEM WAS TOM?
N-N-NEITHER.
I DUNNO WHO *THEY* WERE.

SLAM!
WHICH ONE OF THEM?
N-N-NEITHER.
I DUNNO WHO...
NORA, IS THAT YOU?
WHERE ARE YOU?
NORA!
TOM?
TOM, THOMAS, TOMMY...
RICH BOY TOM.

OKAY, I'M NOT LOVING THE GHOST THING LIKE I THOUGHT I WOULD.
AAH!
PLEASE ASK HIM TO WAIT.
TELL HIM I'VE BEEN DELAYED.
PLEASE...
LEAVE US ALONE!
NORA!
TOM?
WHERE ARE YOU?

UHHH--
UGHH!
TOM!
KRIISH!
BAM!
PLINK!
SLAM!
WHAT'S HAPPENING?!
KRINK!
TOM,
TOM,
TOM...
...BEEN
DELAYED...
WHERE
ARE YOU?
PLEASE,
LEAVE US
ALONE!
REEOOO
WWR!!!

TOM, WHAT IS THAT THING?
I HAVE NO IDEA.
YOU'VE NEVER SEEN IT BEFORE?
DO YOU THINK WE COULD DISCUSS THIS ANOTHER TIME?
SHE'S RIGHT.
RUN!!

HELP!
RUN!
AAAAAH!!
GO! GO! GO!
WHAT IS GOING ON?
GO DOWN, GO DOWN!

IT'S QUIET UP THERE NOW.
DIDN'T YOU GUYS HEAR *ANYTHING* BEFORE?
NO, WE JUST HEARD YOU RUNNING AND YELLING.
THERE'S NO SUCH THING AS GHOSTS.
HMPH.
I THINK YOU GIRLS FREAKED YOURSELVES OUT...
DAD, THEY DIDN'T IMAGINE IT.
WE'VE SEEN THE GHOSTS TOO.
WHEN WE WERE COMING DOWN THE STAIRS, THERE WAS SOMEONE WITH US.
I DON'T THINK YOU SAW HIM.
I WANT YOU TO MEET HIM NOW.
HE SAYS IT'S EASIER FOR HIM TO APPEAR TO US. US KIDS, I MEAN.
BUT HE'S GOING TO TRY TO MAKE YOU SEE HIM.

MOM, DAD, MR. JAMES, THIS IS TOM.
OH. MY...
HE'S NOT ONE OF THE BAD GHOSTS. ARE YOU?
NO. I'M VERY PLEASED TO MEET YOU, MR. AND MRS. REILLY.
MOM, HE STAYED IN THE HOUSE TO TAKE CARE OF HIS MOTHER.
NOW HE CAN'T LEAVE.
OH, HOW SAD.

THE... THE OTHER GHOSTS--
WHO ARE THEY?
THE WOMAN'S NAME IS INGE.
INGE?
I REMEMBER INGE. SHE WORKED FOR MY MOTHER.
I DON'T KNOW WHO THEY OTHERS ARE, BUT I KNOW THEY'RE ANGRY. NO DOUBT THEY THINK YOU'RE THE INTRUDERS.
DO YOU THINK WE'RE INTRUDERS, TOM?
NO, SIR.
YOUR FAMILY BELONGS IN THIS HOUSE.
RIGHT.
THIS IS OUR HOUSE.
AND *WE'RE* NOT LEAVING.
I AM.
OUR HOUSE.
WE'RE NOT LEAVING.

Chapter 5:
GHOST HUNTING

I CAN FEEL YOU MORE STRONGLY NOW.
I KNOW.
ME TOO.
DO YOU WANT TO...?
I THINK WE SHOULD TRY, AT LEAST.

I HAVE TO TELL YOU SOMETHING.
THERE'S THIS TV SHOW, *SPIRIT SEEKERS INTERNATIONAL.*
THEY HAVE ALL THIS SPECIAL EQUIPMENT TO HUNT GHOSTS.
DON'T LAUGH.
THEY'RE COMING HERE TOMORROW.
MY PARENTS CALLED THE SHOW'S PRODUCERS.
THEY WON'T BE ABLE TO DRIVE YOU OUT, EXORCISE YOU, OR SOMETHING, WILL THEY?
I'LL STAY OUT OF THEIR WAY.
THEY WON'T BE ABLE TO MAKE YOU GO AWAY?
DEFINITELY NOT.

GOOD.
EVEN IF YOU WANTED TO LEAVE, I WOULDN'T LET YOU.
OH, IS THAT RIGHT?
DO YOU KNOW WHAT I WISH?
I WISH WE COULD GO OUT FOR A WALK.
I COULD SHOW YOU EVERYTHING THAT'S CHANGED IN THE NEIGHBORHOOD.
WE COULD WALK ALL THE WAY DOWN TO THE RIVER...
...AND THEN HAVE DINNER ON GRAND AVENUE.
IT WOULD BE A *REAL* DATE.

THAT CAME OUT SO WRONG!
IT'S ALL RIGHT...
NO! I DIDN'T MEAN IT HOW IT SOUNDED AT ALL.
I'M HAPPY STAYING HERE WITH YOU.
I KNOW.
YOU'RE RIGHT, THOUGH THESE AFTERNOONS WE SPEND TOGETHER, THEY AREN'T REAL DATES.
NOT WHAT A MODERN GIRL EXPECTS.
BUT IF I TRY TO LEAVE THE HOUSE...THERE'S NOTHING ON THE OTHER SIDE OF THE DOOR BUT BLACKNESS.
NOT BLACKNESS... NOTHINGNESS.
THE END OF EVERYTHING.
I DON'T CARE THAT WE HAVE TO STAY IN.
OKAY?
OKAY.

IF YOU COULD SIGN THIS RELEASE HERE.
AND THEN THIS ONE AT THE BOTTOM.
THEN SIGN THE RELEASES FOR ALL THREE MINOR CHILDREN.
GREAT. THAT'LL MAKE OUR LAWYERS HAPPY.
YOU'RE EILEEN, RIGHT?
HAVE YOU SEEN THE GHOST?
YEAH.
THEY'RE NOT OUR FRIENDS ANYMORE.
THAT'S WHAT I HEAR.
WE'RE GOING TO TRY TO FIND OUT WHAT THEY WANT.
MAYBE THEN THEY'LL GO AWAY.

REIKO!
HAVE WE WIRED THE UPSTAIRS YET?
ALL DONE.
WE HAVE CAMERAS ON THE HALLWAY AND ON THE OLDER DAUGHTER'S BEDROOM.
JEAN, WHERE ARE THESE CATS OF YOURS?
THEY'RE OUT ON THE SUNPORCH.
THEY WON'T COME IN THE HOUSE ANYMORE.
COLE, CAN WE GET A CAMERA ON THE CATS?
SUNPORCH.
WHO'S GOT THE DIGITAL VOICE RECORDERS?
HAS ANYONE TAKEN BASELINE READINGS IN THE BASEMENT YET?
I'M ON IT.
WE'RE GOING DARK IN TEN!
THE CAMERAS ARE GOING TO START ROLLING.
JUST...BE YOURSELVES.

WELCOME TO *SPIRIT SEEKERS INTERNATIONAL.*
I'M JEFF MARKAWAY.
AND I'M SALLY MARKAWAY.
REC

WE'RE IN ST. PAUL, MINNESOTA, WITH THE REILLY FAMILY AND THE *SPIRIT SEEKERS* TEAM.
THE REILLYS MOVED INTO THIS BEAUTIFUL VICTORIAN HOME A FEW MONTHS AGO.
BUT THEY'VE DISCOVERED THAT THEY'RE NOT ALONE HERE.
REC

WE'RE GOING TO TRY TO HELP THE FAMILY BY MAKING SOME PARANORMAL CONNECTIONS.
READY? LET'S FIND SOME GHOSTS.
REC

LOTS OF CONSTRUCTION GOING ON HERE.
THAT CAN DISTURB SPIRITS.
YEAH, THEY DON'T LIKE CHANGE.
REC
MAN, I HOPE WE SEE HALF OF WHAT THE KIDS SAW.
THEIR STORY IS AMAZING.
REC
DID YOU JUST HEAR SOMETHING?
NO.
MAYBE.
WHAT WAS IT?
REC
YOU OPEN IT.
I'M NOT GOING TO OPEN IT. YOU OPEN IT.
NO, I'M NOT GOING TO OPEN IT.
REC
THIS IS THE OLDEST DAUGHTER'S ROOM.
SHE INTERACTED WITH A DARK ENTITY THAT COULD BE AN ELEMENTAL SPIRIT.
REC
HELLO?
WE'RE LOOKING FOR THE TWO MEN IN WORK CLOTHES.
DID YOU LIVE IN THIS HOUSE?
IS THERE SOME REASON YOU DON'T WANT TO LEAVE?
NOTHING.
HOPE SALLY AND CARIN ARE HAVING BETTER LUCK.
REC

WE HEARD THAT YOU KNOCKED DOWN ONE OF THE KIDS WHO LIVES HERE.
CAN YOU TELL US WHY YOU DID THAT?
REC
IF YOU TALK INTO THIS LITTLE MACHINE HERE, IT'LL RECORD YOUR VOICE.
REC
HELLO?
ANYONE?
REC
INGE?
INGE, WE UNDERSTAND THAT YOU'RE WORRIED ABOUT MEETING SOMEONE.
REC
WHO ARE YOU MEETING?
CAN YOU TELL US ABOUT IT?
REC

WE'RE GOING TO TRY ONE MORE THING BEFORE WE LEAVE.
IT'S AN OLD TRICK.
REC

I'M GOING TO THROW THIS BALL DOWN THE HALLWAY...
...AND HOPE THAT ONE OF THE GHOSTS THROWS IT BACK.
REC

NOTHING.
ALL RIGHT.
I'LL GO GET THE BALL.

I HEARD IT STOP BOUNCING.
WHERE IS IT?

WE'LL REVIEW ALL OUR AUDIO AND VIDEOTAPES AND GET BACK TO YOU IN A COUPLE OF DAYS.
THAT'LL BE GREAT.
BUT YOU DIDN'T SEE ANYTHING?
NO. THAT'S HOW IT GOES SOMETIMES.
THE GHOSTS DON'T WANT TO COME OUT AND--
BOUNCE
BOUNCE
--PLAY.
THAT WOULD HAVE MADE A GREAT FINAL SHOT.

MORE VISITORS?
WHO ARE THEY?
MY MOM WANTS TO TRY OLD-FASHIONED PSYCHICS, SINCE *SPIRIT SEEKERS* DIDN'T FIND ANYTHING WITH THEIR EQUIPMENT LAST WEEK.
SHE PHONED SOME PSYCHIC SOCIETY NUMBER SHE GOT FROM MY FLAKY GUIDANCE COUNSELOR.
FLAKY.
BACK INTO HIDING FOR ME, I SUPPOSE.
IT'S JUST ...WE CAN'T LIVE HERE WITH THOSE *OTHER* GHOSTS.
I KNOW.
GO.
I'LL SEE YOU LATER.

I AM BETTINA DUDLEY.
THESE ARE SAMUEL SANDERSON AND KATHERINE HILL.

WE EACH HAVE SUCH VERY DIFFERENT APPROACHES.
FRANKLY, I DON'T KNOW WHY THE PSYCHICAL SOCIETY SENT US ALL TOGETHER.

AND WHO IS THIS?
THIS IS NORA. MY OLDEST.
TEENAGERS ARE A POWERFUL SOURCE OF PSYCHIC ENERGY.
SPIRITS ARE DRAWN TO THE LIFE FORCE OF YOUTH.

YES, WELL, WE DON'T KNOW THAT THERE ARE ACTUALLY ANY SPIRITS HERE.

LIKE PEOPLE, HOUSES CAN BECOME ILL, UNBALANCED.
IN MY PRACTICE, I CURE THE HOUSE.
HEAL ITS ENERGY.

JEAN, WAS THIS HOUSE BUILT ON ANY LEY LINES?
I DON'T KNOW.

THE REAL ESTATE AGENT NEVER MENTIONED--

LEY LINES ARE PATHS OF MYSTICAL ENERGY.
THEY HAVE NOTHING TO DO WITH REAL ESTATE.

HAVE YOU SEEN ANYTHING?
GHOSTS?
DANCING SKELETONS?
FLAMING SKULLS?
ANY OF THE USUAL STUFF?
MY MOM SAID NOT TO TELL YOU ANY DETAILS.
THAT WAY WE'LL KNOW IF YOU'RE GENUINE.
HAHA!
FAIR ENOUGH.
WHAT ARE YOU TWO CHATTING ABOUT BACK THERE?
LET'S ALL TRY TO STAY ON THE SAME WAVELENGTH, KATHERINE.
FAT CHANCE OF THAT, BETTINA.

THE CHILDREN SAW THE APPARITIONS UP HERE?
IF THEY SAW APPARITIONS...
YES, SAMUEL.
I CAN SHOW YOU THE EXACT SPOT.

WHO ARE YOU?
YES, I'LL TELL HIM TO WAIT.
POOR INGE.

THERE IS NEGATIVE ENERGY IN THIS HOUSE, JEAN.
BUT I DON'T BELIEVE HUMAN SPIRITS ARE TRAPPED WITHIN THESE WALLS.

I THINK YOU'RE WRONG ABOUT THAT, BETTINA.

I'VE BEEN CURING HOUSES FOR FIFTEEN YEARS.

I AM A CERTIFIED VORTEX SPECIALIST.
NOT TO MENTION BEING A NATURAL SENSITIVE.

AND I CAN TELL YOU THAT THERE ARE NO GHOSTS IN THIS HOUSE!
OH!
GET OUT.

PLEASE TAKE A DRINK, BETTINA.
TAKE MY NUMBER.
I HAVE A FEELING YOU'LL NEED IT.
GOODNESS.
WELL, AT LEAST THEY DIDN'T FOLLOW US DOWN--
KEE-RACK
AIIIEEE!!

MOM!
STOP IT!
STOP IT!
WE ALL NEED TO GET OUT OF THIS HOUSE.
GOOD IDEA.
WE'RE HOME!
WHAT'S--
I'LL EXPLAIN LATER.
OUT!

NORA THERESE REILLY, GET IN THIS CAR.
CREEEAK.
CLICK

Chapter 6:
CROSSING OVER
INDICATOR SPECIES
This is Your Planet

HEY.
HI.
HI, NICK.
SO, I DIDN'T SEE YOU AT REHEARSALS YESTERDAY.
OH, YEAH. I COULDN'T MAKE IT.
THERE'S STUFF GOING ON AT HOME.
YEAH, JAMILA SAID YOU'RE STAYING AT YOUR AUNT'S.
SO... MAYBE YOU'D LIKE TO ESCAPE FOR A WHILE.
ESCAPE?
YEAH. WE COULD...
GO FOR A WALK DOWN BY THE RIVER.
MAYBE GET SOMETHING TO EAT.

OH--
NOT AS A DATE...
I KNOW YOU HAVE A BOYFRIEND.
THAT'S SO SWEET, NICK.
I MEAN IT.
BUT...?

BUT...I HAVE TO GO SEE SOMEONE IN MINNEAPOLIS.
OH.

JUST A FRIEND.
BUT...I... HAVE TO GET GOING.

SEE YA.

Two Down
Coffee Shop

Archer Corporation
Katherine Hill
Senior Technical Writer

If you need anything, call me at
home: 651-555-6709
Two Down Coffee Shop
356 Third Street

THERE YOU ARE!
LET'S GO IN.

THEY HAVE THE BEST HOT CHOCOLATE HERE.
MY MOM SAYS HOT CHOCOLATE SOLVES EVERYTHING.
THANKS FOR MEETING ME.
WHY COULDN'T WE TALK OVER THE PHONE?
UM...
IS IT YOUR PARENTS?
THEY DIDN'T WANT YOU TO CONTACT ME?
NO, THAT'S NOT--
I MEAN, THEY DON'T EVEN KNOW I WANT TO TALK TO YOU.
I'VE BEEN GOING TO THE HOUSE WHEN THEY THINK I'M AT PLAY REHEARSALS.
YOU'RE GOING BACK TO THAT HOUSE ON YOUR OWN?
IT'S NOT SAFE.
I HAVE TO.
I HAVE TO BE THERE.

YOU KNOW, I WAS REALLY PSYCHED TO VISIT THE HOME OF ELEANOR HAYS.
I WAS A BIG FAN OF HERS IN COLLEGE. HAVE YOU READ *THE UNCLEARED FIELD?*
IT'S A GHOST STORY. LITERARY SCHOLARS SAY THAT IT'S BASED ON SOMETHING THAT HAPPENED IN HER FAMILY...
...THE DEATH OF AN UNCLE NAMED TOM, LONG BEFORE SHE WAS BORN.
YES, I KNOW THE STORY.
I THOUGHT MAYBE YOU DID.
YOU'RE GOING BACK THERE TO SEE TOM.
I NEED TO BE WITH HIM.
WITH THOSE OTHER GHOSTS AROUND, EVERYTHING'S MESSED UP.
I DON'T KNOW WHAT TO DO.

CAN YOU HELP ME?
WELL, I CAN'T LET YOU TRY TO CLEAN THAT HOUSE ON YOUR OWN.
SO...DO WE HOLD A SÉANCE OR WHAT?
NOPE. NOTHING THAT EXCITING. YET.
WE START AT THE LIBRARY.
THE LIBRARY?
WE HAVE TO HELP THE GHOSTS MOVE ON TO THE AFTERLIFE.
BUT TO DO THAT, WE HAVE TO UNDERSTAND WHO THEY WERE WHEN THEY WERE ALIVE.
LET'S GET STARTED.

GONG
GONG
GONG
WHERE HAVE YOU BEEN?!
IT'S BEEN DAYS!
I KNOW. I'M SORRY.
BUT I HAVE SO MUCH TO SHOW YOU.
I'VE BEEN AT THE LIBRARY. AND AT THE HISTORICAL SOCIETY.
THERE'S SO MUCH STUFF THERE--IT'S AMAZING.
I KNOW WHO THEY ARE!
YOU KNOW WHO *WHO* ARE?

THE GHOSTS, OF COURSE.
INGE OLSEN. I KNOW WHO SHE IS, OR WAS. I KNOW HER *STORY.*
AND PETER USHER AND LLOYD DUDLEY.

BACK IN THE 1930s, DURING THE DEPRESSION, THE RUTHERFORDS--
--YOUR SISTER AND HER HUSBAND--
--TOOK IN BOARDERS, MOSTLY PEOPLE WHO WERE OUT OF WORK.
DO YOU REMEMBER THAT?
NOT REALLY.

TWO OF THOSE BOARDERS WERE PETER AND LLOYD.
ONE NIGHT THEY GOT INTO A FIGHT WITH SOME RICH GUYS.
SEE? BOTH PETER AND LLOYD *DIED VIOLENTLY.*
THAT'S ONE OF THE REASONS PEOPLE BECOME GHOSTS.
TWO MEN KILLED IN PRIOR PARK
THE VICTIMS HAVE BEEN IDENTIFIED AS PETER USHER AND LLOYD DUDLEY
NO CHARGES IN PRIOR PARK CASE
Police Chief Calls Off Investigation

LLOYD WAS FROM SOME LITTLE TOWN DOWN BY NORTHFIELD.
DEATH NOTICES
In Le Sueur, Thomas Carlin, aged
BARNES—eighteen years, son of Thomas Joseph Barnes
and Minerva (née Carlin) of St. Paul, and elder
brother of Joan Amelia, in a horseback riding
accident. Tom, as he was fondly called, was to
attend the University of Chicago in the
autumn. His dreams were many, and vivid all,
about what was to come. Now he dreams in
peace forever, always happy, always young.
Friends are invited to the funeral service to
be held July 24 at 11:00 o'clock a.m. Burial at
River Grove Cemetery.
Now he dreams in
peace forever, always happy, always young.
WHY DID YOU DIG ALL THIS UP?

THAT'S WHAT I'VE BEEN TELLING YOU.
WE CAN USE THIS INFORMATION TO REACH THE OTHER GHOSTS...
...TO HELP THEM MOVE ON.
WHAT DO YOU THINK?
TOM, TALK TO ME.
IT SOUNDS LIKE A GOOD PLAN.
NOT FLAKY AT ALL.
ONCE THE OTHER GHOSTS ARE GONE, MY FAMILY CAN MOVE BACK IN.
AND EVERYTHING WILL BE NORMAL AGAIN.
TOMORROW.
IT'LL ALL BE OVER TOMORROW.
TOMORROW.
OKAY.

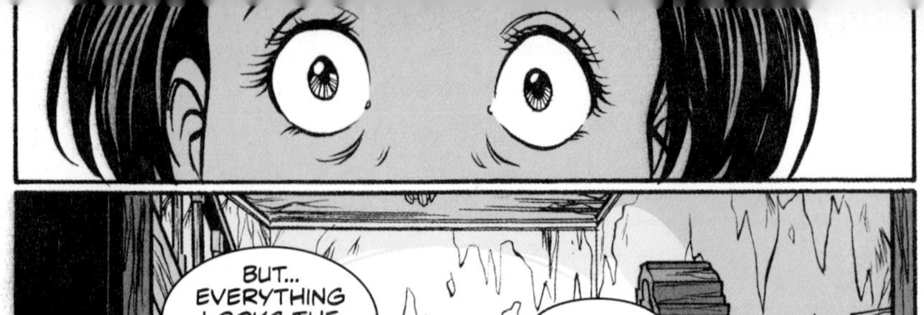

BUT... EVERYTHING LOOKS THE SAME FROM OUTSIDE.
YEAH.
IT'S JUST INSIDE. UPSTAIRS IS WORSE, BUT WE DON'T GO UP THERE ANYMORE.

UM... DID YOU WANT TO MEET TOM?
HE'S--
BEHIND ME. YEAH, I KNOW.
RIGHT. BECAUSE YOU'RE--
PSYCHIC.
YEP.

TOM. PLEASED TO MEET YOU.
DON'T MIND ME.
I'M JUST A LITTLE...I'VE NEVER SEEN A HOUSE TAKEN OVER BY THE SPIRIT WORLD LIKE THIS.
LOOKS LIKE WE HAVE OUR WORK CUT OUT FOR US.

...AND IF ANYTHING GOES WRONG, JUST GET OUT OF THE HOUSE, OKAY?
NOT THAT ANYTHING WILL GO WRONG. REMEMBER THAT LIVING BEINGS HAVE MUCH MORE ENERGY AND POWER THAN--
KATHERINE, YOU CAME BACK!
INGE! WE WERE JUST ABOUT--
PLEASE HELP ME.
THE DARKNESS IS GETTING STRONGER. I THINK IT WILL SWALLOW ME.
I DON'T WANT TO BE IN THIS PLACE ANYMORE.
THEN THIS IS YOUR TIME TO PASS ON, INGE.
THINK, THINK HARD ABOUT WHO WAS WAITING FOR YOU.
I DON'T...I CAN'T REMEMBER HIS NAME...
TRY. WHERE WERE YOU TRYING TO GET TO THAT DAY?
I COULDN'T GO OUT.
MY NECK HURT SO MUCH, AND THE MISSUS SAID I HAD A FEVER.
I TRIED TO GET A MESSAGE TO HIM, A MESSAGE TO...TO...

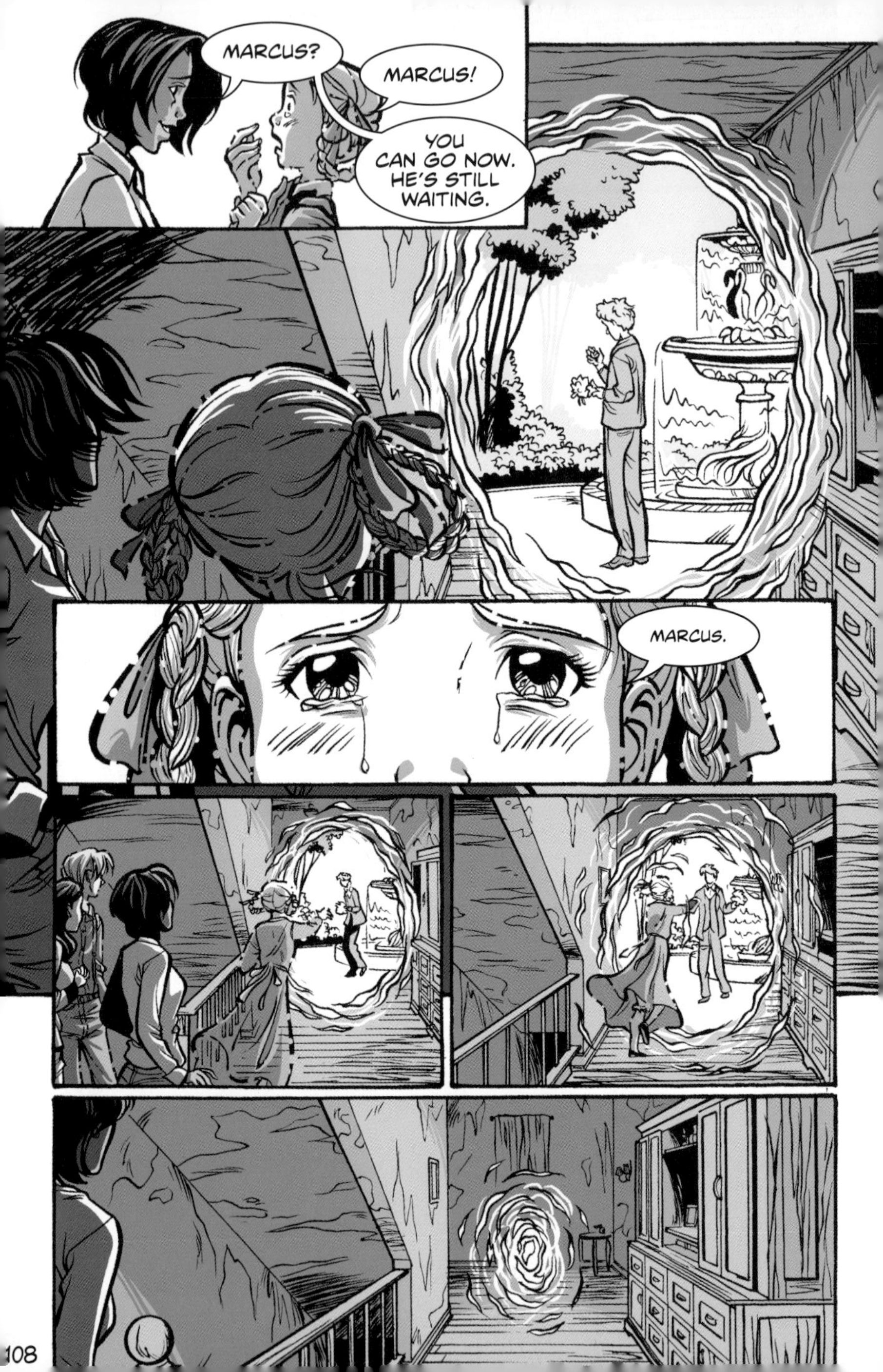
MARCUS?
MARCUS!
YOU CAN GO NOW. HE'S STILL WAITING.
MARCUS.

WOW. THAT WAS AMAZING.
AND SO *EASY.*
INGE *WANTED* TO GO.
I DON'T THINK THE OTHERS WILL BE THAT EASY.
BUT THEY *WILL* WANT TO GO, ONCE WE REMIND THEM ABOUT THEIR PAST LIVES.
AND WHAT ABOUT THAT THING...THAT BLACK CLOUD THAT ATTACKED US?
I THINK IT FEEDS OFF THE NEGATIVE ENERGY OF THE OTHERS.
WE'LL DEAL WITH THAT ONE LAST.
FIRST, WE HAVE TO FIND THE BOYS.
PETER! LLOYD!
SHOW YOUR UGLY MUGS!

YOU'RE GOING TO MAKE THEM MAD!
NORA, THESE TWO WON'T COME OUT TO HAVE A NICE CHAT WITH US.
WE HAVE TO MAKE THEM ANGRY TO GET THEM TO MANIFEST.
OKAY...
COME ON OUT, YOU LOSERS! WHAT ARE YOU AFRAID OF?
SHOW YOUR MUGS, YOU NO-ACCOUNT BUMS--
I WAS NEVER NO BUM!
I ALWAYS PAID MY OWN WAY. BUT THEY WERE AGAINST ME-- ALL OF 'EM!
THEY DIDN'T KNOW YOU, LLOYD. THEY DIDN'T UNDERSTAND YOU.
BUT THERE MUST HAVE BEEN PEOPLE WHO DID.

THINK, LLOYD.
I KNOW IT'S REALLY HARD TO FIND A GOOD MOMENT IN YOUR LIFE...
BUT THERE WERE SOME.
LLOYD, LOOK.
THAT'S HOME, ISN'T IT? WHERE YOU GREW UP? A FARM, WHERE PEOPLE RESPECT HARD WORK?
LET GO OF THIS SHADOW LIFE.
HOW SOFT DO YOU THINK I AM?
YOU THINK I DON'T KNOW WHAT YOU'RE DOING?
YOU'RE TRYING TO DRIVE ME OUT.
JUST SWEEP ME OUT WITH THE DIRT.
JUST RENT OUT OUR ROOM TO THE NEXT PAIR OF BUMS, RIGHT?

I WON'T GO...
I WON'T GO...
NOOOO...
IT TOOK HIM!
HE'S ***GONE.***
I COULD FEEL IT. HE WAS SO FURIOUS HE GAVE THE CLOUD ENOUGH ENERGY TO ***SWALLOW*** HIM. HE'S--
KATHERINE!

NO...
TOM, WHAT DO WE DO?!
THERE'S STILL A CHANCE... I MIGHT BE ABLE TO SAVE HER.
BUT YOU HAVE TO LEAVE. NOW.
NO WAY.
I AM NOT LEAVING THIS HOUSE.
ARGH, YOU'RE A STUBBORN WOMAN.
GO DOWNSTAIRS AND WAIT BY THE FRONT DOOR. DO YOU HEAR ME?

YES, DEAR.
I DON'T WANT ANYTHING TO HAPPEN TO YOU.
I KNOW.
DITTO.
BE CAREFUL.
I WANT YOU BACK.

KATHERINE!
TOM!
WHERE ARE WE? I COULDN'T FIND MY WAY OUT...
WE HAVE TO FIND A WEAK SPOT IN THE WALL AND PUSH THROUGH.
I GUESS THE CLOUD CAN'T DIGEST THE LIVING.
BUT, TOM, THE DANGER TO YOU...I TOLD YOU I COULD FEEL IT. LLOYD IS GONE COMPLETELY.
NO GHOST, NO SPIRIT, NO AFTERLIFE. CONSUMED. TURNED INTO PURE ANGER.
...DREAMS IN PEACE FOREVER...
WHERE HAVE YOU BEEN?
I MISS YOU SO MUCH...
THAT CAME OUT SO WRONG!
...ALWAYS HAPPY, ALWAYS YOUNG...
DON'T BE AFRAID. DON'T FEED IT ANY ENERGY. THINK OF...
NORA.
AAAIIIIEEE!
IT'S GONE!
LET'S GET OUT OF THIS PLACE.
WHAT WAS THAT YOU SAID ABOUT FINDING A WEAK SPOT?

TOM?
KATHERINE?
SORRY TOM, BUT I CAN'T WAIT DOWNSTAIRS WITH THAT *THING* ON THE LOOSE.
LOOKING FOR ME, PRINCESS?
UHHH!
ARE YOU GOING TO CONJURE UP A SWEET MEMORY FOR ME?
REMIND ME OF A PRETTY SCENE FROM THE GOOD OLD DAYS?
I HAVE A PRETTY SCENE RIGHT HERE.
YOU KNOW, YOU AND I COULD BE TOGETHER FOREVER.
YOU BETTER WATCH IT, OR I'LL CALL FOR TOM.

HE'LL NEVER FIND US. HE COULDN'T FIND *ME* FOR MORE THAN SEVENTY-FIVE YEARS.
HE'S AN IDIOT.

WELL... HE CAN BE QUITE A BORE.

OH, I KNOW.
AND YOU'RE MUCH BETTER LOOKING.

OF COURSE I AM.

BUT I *CAN'T*.

WHY NOT?

MY FATHER WOULD NEVER ALLOW IT.
A BOY LIKE YOU? HE'D BE FUR--

A BOY LIKE ME?
WHAT AM I *LIKE*, PRINCESS?

MY FATHER IS QUITE WELL-OFF. HE'S A LAWYER, YOU KNOW.
AND YOU'RE... WELL, YOU'RE A COMMON LABORER.
YOU DIE, AND WHO CARES? YOU'RE A *NOBODY!*

COMMON?!
A NOBODY, AM I?
I'M SMARTER THAN ALL OF YOU TOGETHER.

YOU WEREN'T SMART ENOUGH TO SEE THAT COMING.
IF I'M GOING, I'LL TAKE YOU WITH ME!
NO! LET GO!
NORA!
LET HER GO, YOU MONSTER!
AAAIIIEEEE!!
...DON'T WANT ANYTHING TO HAPPEN TO YOU...
I WANT YOU BACK.
IT'S FADING AWAY...?
THERE'S NO MORE RAGE IN THE HOUSE.
...THERE'S ANOTHER DREAM CALLING OUT...
NORA.

LISTEN!
WHAT? WHAT DO YOU HEAR?!
NOTHING.
NO CREEPY WHISPERING BLACK CLOUD.
NO PETER AND LLOYD STOMPING AROUND.
WE CLEANED THIS HOUSE *GOOD.*
WELL, NOT THAT GOOD.
WHAT DO YOU MEAN?
DON'T TELL ME MORE GHOSTS ARE HIDING SOMEWHERE.
JUST THE ONE, NORA.
I HAVE TO GO.

NO. THAT WAS *NOT* PART OF THE PLAN.
YOU BELONG IN THIS HOUSE.
I BELONGED HERE ONCE, A LONG TIME AGO.
NOW I BELONG SOMEWHERE ELSE.
I'M GOING TO GO...
BE ELSEWHERE FOR A FEW MINUTES.
I FEEL LIKE I FINALLY HAD A CHANCE TO LIVE.
I HAD A CHANCE TO FALL IN LOVE, LIKE MY SISTER HAD...
AND I CAN GO. WITH NO REGRETS.
WILL YOU SHOW ME THE WAY?
I CAN'T.
PLEASE?
I WANT YOU TO HELP ME.

I WILL MISS YOU EVERY DAY.
IF THERE'S A WAY, I'LL SEE YOU AGAIN.
ON THE OTHER SIDE.
I KNOW WHAT YOU NEED TO CROSS OVER.
I KNOW YOUR WHOLE LIFE'S STORY.
YOU NEED TO THINK OF THEM...
YOUR FAMILY.
IT'S TIME YOU JOINED THEM.
RUFF!!

BLACKIE!
THAT'S MY DOG.
YOU DID IT! THANK YOU.
I LOVE YOU, NORA REILLY.
I LOVE YOU, TOM BARNES.
I'LL SEE YOU AGAIN.
SOMEDAY.
SOMEDAY.

TAP
TAP
TAP
NORA, CAN YOU HELP ME?
WHAT ARE YOU TYPING?
REVISIONS ON A PLAY I WROTE FOR THE SPRING DRAMA FESTIVAL.
ARE YOU GOING TO STAR IN IT?
NO, I'M THE WRITER AND DIRECTOR.
JAMILA'S GOING TO STAR IN IT.
OH.
THAT BOY IS BACK.

WHAT BOY?
THAT BOY WHO LIKES YOU.
YOU'VE SEEN HIM AGAIN?
WHERE?
OUT IN THE BACKYARD.
HE'S PLAYING WITH AIDAN AND HIS FRIENDS.
SEE?

HI, NICK!
DID YOU--
OOOMPH!!
HA HAHA HA!
WHOA.
SORRY ABOUT THAT!
OH, NOT AS SORRY AS YOU'RE GOING TO BE.
WHUMP
THUMP
HEY.
HEY.
DO YOU WANT TO COME INSIDE FOR SOME HOT CHOCOLATE?
I'VE BEEN TOLD THERE ARE FEW PROBLEMS THAT CAN'T BE SOLVED BY HOT CHOCOLATE.
THE END.

QUESTIONS AND ANSWERS

I'D HAVE ONCE SAID THAT NO SANE PERSON WOULD EVER ASK ME FOR ROMANTIC ADVICE. BUT YOU DON'T DATE A GHOST WITHOUT LEARNING A FEW THINGS.

CHRIS: Are you sorry you wasted so much time with Tom when you could've been with Nick the whole time?

NORA: Not at all! I don't think I wasted any time with Tom. It was great getting to know him. He was an excellent person to fall in love with. So even though it couldn't last—no, I don't regret it at all. By the time I started dating Nick, I felt as if I'd learned a lot about myself. So the timing was perfect.

LIANNA: Have you ever tried to contact Tom again? Like, psychically?

NORA: No. Tom has moved on to where he should be. I wouldn't ever try to disturb that. I believe, in my heart, that he's happy now. And so am I!

BREE: My best friend thinks I'm making a mistake going out with a certain guy. Like how Kirsty didn't want you to date Tom. I don't want to have to choose between my best friend and my boyfriend. What do I do?

NORA: Kirsty and I—and Jamila, too—see things from way different points of view sometimes. But that's good—we can give one another reality checks. But you have to trust your own instincts too. Could your friend be afraid of losing you? That feeling can be scarier than a houseful of angry ghosts. Or could she be making some good points about this guy, things she can see because she's looking at him from the outside? Think about what's a good point and what's exaggeration, and let her know you know she has your best interests at heart. After all, she's your best friend!

ABOUT THE AUTHOR AND THE ARTIST

ANN KERNS has edited many nonfiction books for young readers and is the author of *Australia in Pictures, Romania in Pictures, Martha Stewart, Troy, Who Will Shout If Not Us?: Student Activists and the Tiananmen Square Protest,* and *Did Castles Have Bathrooms?: And Other Questions about the Middle Ages.* She enjoys reading, travel, cooking, and music. A native of Illinois, she is a transplant to Minneapolis.

JANINA GÖRRISSEN was born in Frankenthal, Germany, and studied comic arts in Barcelona, Spain. Her works include *Black Is for Beginnings* from Flux and the first book in the My Boyfriend Is a Monster series, *I Love Him to Pieces* by Evonne Tsang. Her website is jgoerrissen.com.